The NOSE BOOK

BY AL PERKINS

ILLUSTRATED BY

Roy McKie

A Bright & Early Book

RANDOM HOUSE/NEW YORK

This title was originally catalogued by the Library of Congress as follows:

Perkins, Al.
The nose book. Illustrated by Roy McKie. New York,
Random House ₁1970₁.

₁28₁ p. col. illus. 24 cm. (A Bright & early book, BE8) $1.95

Noses are interesting and serve many purposes including the one
of holding up glasses.

₁1. Stories in rhyme₁   I. McKie, Roy, illus. II. Title.

PZ8.3.P42No   [E]   71–117540
ISBN 0-394–80623–9   MARC

Library of Congress   71 ₁7₁   A C

Trade Ed.: ISBN: 0-**394-80623-9**   Lib. Ed.: ISBN: 0-**394-90623-3**

Everybody
grows
a nose.

I see a nose
on every face.

I see noses
every place!

A nose
between
each pair of eyes.

Noses!
Noses!
Every size.

They grow
on every
kind of head.

They come in blue . . .

. . . and pink

. . . and red.

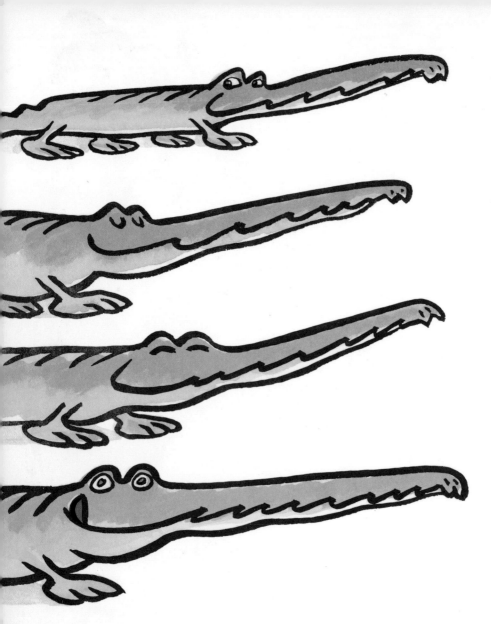

Some are
very, very long.

Some are
very, very strong.

Everywhere a fellow goes,
he sees some
new, new kind of nose.

A nose is useful.
After all . . .

some play horns . . .

. . . and some play ball.

A nose is good
for making holes
. . . in trees

. . . and roofs

. . . and barber poles.

But sometimes
noses aren't much fun.
They sniffle.

They get burned by sun.

A nose gets punched . . .

. . . and bumped on doors

. . . and bumped on walls

. . . and bumped on floors!

Sometimes
your nose
will make you sad.
Sometimes
your nose
will make you mad.

BUT . . .

Just suppose
you had no nose!

Then you
could never
smell
a rose . . .

. . . or pie, or chicken a la king.

You'd never smell a single thing.

And one thing more.
Suppose . . . no nose . . .

Where would
all our glasses sit?
They'd all fall off!
Just THINK of it!

And that's why
everybody grows,
between his eyes,
some kind of nose!